*Praise for*

# MASTERPLANS

"In this debut, Nick Almeida offers prose both precise and startling, stories that provide surprise upon surprise. Masterplans is a hilarious and original collection. This is the work of a bold and sure new writer."

—**Toni Jensen**, author of *Carry* and *From the Hilltop*

"There's more of the stuff of life packed into this little chapbook than you're going to find in pretty much any novel you might read this year. The title story is nothing less than a masterpiece, and every story here pulses and thrums with humor, heartbreak, terror, charm, and wry, hard-won wisdom. Nick Almeida has written a stunner of a debut, and I can't wait to see what this lavishly gifted young writer delivers next."

—**Ben Fountain**, author of *Billy Lynn's Long Halftime Walk* and *Beautiful Country Burn Again*

# ■ MAJTERPLANJ

# MASTERPLANS

## NICK ALMEIDA

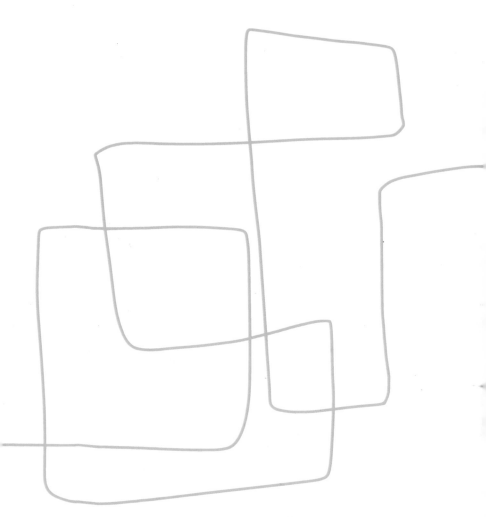

# MASTERPLANS

## NICK ALMEIDA

To receive new fiction, contest deadlines,
and other curated content right to
your inbox, send an email to
newsletter@mastersreview.com

*Masterplans*
by Nick Almeida
Selected by Steve Almond
Edited by Cole Meyer

Art Concept by Kyle Schwander
Front cover design by Chelsea Wales
Interior design by Cynthia Young

First printing.

ISBN: 978-1-7363695-2-4

Printed in the USA

To receive new fiction, contest deadlines,
and other curated content right to your inbox,
send an email to newsletter@mastersreview.com

# ACKNOWLEDGEMENTS

"Gone Elvis" was a winner of *American Literary Review's* "Flash Flood" fiction contest and appeared online.

"Gourd Queen" was the Grand Prize Winner of *The World's Best Short-Short Contest* judged by Robert Olen Butler and appeared in *The Southeast Review.*

"Smoke For The Mozarts" appeared in *Waxwing.*

"How to Shoot Grooms" appeared in *Hunger Mountain.*

# CONTENTS

# EDITOR'S NOTE

The first thing I ever had published was a book review for *The Masters Review*. I was a junior in college and had been reading for the review for about six or seven months when I was offered the opportunity to review this little chapbook from Rose Metal Press, *Ghost Box Evolution in Cadillac, Michigan* by Rosie Forrest. I'd never heard of a chapbook before, except maybe in passing from some of my poet friends, but I loved flash fiction, and I loved the prospect of such a small, intimate collection. I was blown away by Forrest's book, and I've read it again and again since I wrote that first review.

To me, the chapbook is the perfect container for flash fiction. A form so dedicated to compression and brevity, packaged neatly in this small book. One of my first goals for *The Masters Review* when I assumed the editor-in-chief position at the end of 2018 was to create a space for new writers who want to experiment with their work. I pitched the Chapbook Contest as an opportunity for us to read and champion work in a form we wouldn't normally encounter, and I could not be more pleased with the results. All of our finalists spoke to the editorial staff (and judge Steve Almond) in their own unique voices, but Nick Almeida's *Masterplans* grabbed me from the very first lines and never let go.

Whether you are new to chapbooks like I was or experienced with the form, I'm so grateful for your support of emerging writers, and I cannot wait for you to experience Almeida's transformative *Masterplans*.

—*Cole Meyer*
Editor-in-chief

# INTRODUCTION

*Get Ready to Feel the Uncanny*

I kind of love judging writing contests. First (and most regrettably) I love the idea that someone thinks my judgment is worth a hoot. That's always nice. But also: I grew up as a writer in the small press, flinging one manuscript after another into the wishing well of contests and lit magazines. My pal, the poet and essayist Camille Dungy, likes to tell a story about our time together in the salt mines of MFA school. I had managed to publish a couple of stories and assumed, like others in the program, that I was preternaturally talented.

Then she house sat for me one summer and received on my behaf no fewer than one hundred rejections. This was the secret to my success: I submitted constantly, shamelessly. It was tremendously exciting, not just in a lotto ticket sort of way, but because I had the sense that I was participating in the future of American letters, that all the magazines and contests were basically incubators for the next wave of writers.

I like the idea that—some two decades later—I can play a role in identifying and promoting that next wave.

Of course, as inevitably happens when I'm asked to judge *any-thing*, I was left feeling racked by indecision and guilt, my two favorite emotions. I hate the idea that some emerging writer will interpret my sensibility as a measure of their talent. I told all of the finalists of this contest that their manuscripts deserved to be published books, and I meant it.

But I can also tell you the precise moment that I decided to choose Nick Almeida's *Masterplans* (a copy of which you now hold). It comes towards the end of the first story, which, to this point, has offered the curious account of work colleague who shows up at the office dressed in Elvis Presley regalia. Our narrator, clearly discomfited by this sartorial extravagance, proffers the following confession:

> *We are not unique people. Nor are we the beige clichés of the corporate class. We have horrific fears, our children suffer in ways that in certain nights eviscerate us, and once in our childhoods we heard chains rattling from the end of a dark hallway. We recognize and have even described the dangers of othering our colleague. But his Elvis has damaged too much. We have been forced, in the absence of his reasons, to look at ourselves, the origins of our own outrage, and return again (and again) to the individual moments of our distress.*

Mein Gott! What a sudden and shocking revelation. Of our collective anxieties and vulnerabilities and fears, of the manner in which even the pettiest of our judgments pries open portal of truth. I was rocked back in my seat by how abruptly the author casts us from office gossip into the deep rough of personal doubt.

That, my friends, is what I'm always looking for in writing: the danger of self-revelation, of what Freud called *Das Unheimliche* ("the uncanny") those moments in which the familiar becomes strange and versa vice.

Almeida does this over and over. He stages brief, dizzying dramas in which the astonishing comes to feel inevitable. "A whole life can be this way," he writes, at the end of *Gourd Queen*, a piece about a ne'er-do-well brother who flails about on the wedding day of his celebrated sister. "Some blaze forth while you stutter, you guess, you pick your thigh mole through your pocket and wonder, Who is right, Who cares to catch you, Which shoe is the right shoe, and How will I go on?"

The title story of this collection features numerous elements of what I came to think of as the Almeidan universe: a woman with a prosthetic hook for a hand, a water bed rent by sexual hijinx, a deadly cottonmouth, a plane crash. But at its heart—and this is really key to the whole shebang—the author is writing about grief and trauma, how we survive what we live through.

That's the common concern in all these stories, what turns them into a collection rather than just a buffet of the bizarre. Over and over, Almeida is asking: What happens when we get hurt? How do we survive, knowing we must suffer injury and die?

I'm thinking now of the mother and son, both gravely ill, who go shopping for funeral homes in *Can You Paint a Smile?* I'm thinking of this line, in particular, about the mother: "Possibilities smolder behind her eyelids, my mother: yearning for any furnace of interest, of love."

That's what these stories are after here, the burden of hope shouldered amid the fragility of our existence. To quote one of the old masters: *I've gone looking for that feeling everywhere.*

I found it in *Masterplans*, over and over.

Now it's your turn.

—*Steve Almond*
Guest Judge

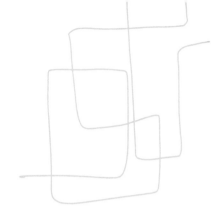

# GONE ELVIS

When we got back to the office after Christmas, word spread quickly: Allen Dennis had gone full Elvis. At first we thought it was a stunt, a gag, but that is not Allen. Allen, are you officiating a wedding? Allen, are you headed to karaoke? He just sat and typed, in his white suit and white belt and wig.

What did this mean? In a biographical sense, for Allen, we formed immediate theories. His wife must've left, a Yuletide jilting, which freed in Allen a locked-away desire for sequins. For gel. The iconic quaffed wig with sideburns: Have you heard about Allen's bodybuilding in the nineties? Obviously he destroyed his hair with steroids. Is he flirting—Margaret from HR posed—with anonymity? There were theories of death, affairs, midlife crises, a dozen seeds from which our Elvis grew. On Fridays, Allen worked from his elderly father's house, he'd explained, where there was an extra desk and his old man who Allen couldn't bear to keep always alone. We lunched at Mamacita's, and, in his absence, deliberated the cause of Allen's Elvis.

Anyone notice the weight? AD had got big AF. Late-era Presley. But why? His unwillingness to share traumas sowed in us a grinding frustration. There were practical concerns, too: What if a client saw? How could vendors take us seriously: Allen in the corner,

1

wearing powder blue sunglasses? We asked in meetings, Allen, did you lose a bet? Allen, are you OK? But there he sat in his usual chair, hiding his stomach beneath a legal pad and suggesting, if it was all right, could we please just move on.

We investigated possible leads. Was this related to the football pool? Had he knocked his head? In the past, Allen solicited the office for his niece's Cancer Walk. This was the most we had ever heard him speak. But the Elvis thing was no such stunt—back then, Allen, our old Allen, who we regard lovingly in retrospect, was not one who liked to be seen. He lunched from a plastic grocery bag at his desk. After layoffs, he requested to move from the bullpen out to the perimeter, which was denied until he made clear that he did not need a desk beside a window.

We are not unique people. Nor are we the beige cliches of the corporate class. We have horrific fears, our children suffer in ways that on certain nights eviscerate us, and once in our childhoods we heard chains rattling from the end of a dark hallway. We recognize and have even described the dangers of othering our colleague. But his Elvis has damaged too much. We have been forced, in the absence of his reasons, to look at ourselves, the origins of our own outrage, and return again (and again) to the individual moments of our distress. Still, Allen reveals only large rings on his hairy pinky fingers, the rhinestones along the welts of his shoes. And in that vacuum of knowing appear our moments, the way the light recedes at the end of a hall, water scalding our mothers, or the words to a faraway song that went like this.

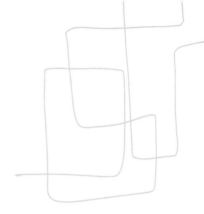

# GOURD QUEEN

My sister has forgotten her shoes. My sister has forgotten her white shoes and is furious. My sister has forgotten her white shoes and is furious at her good-for-nothing bridesmaids, whom she has begun calling *those sweaty hoes*. My sister does not care much for me, either. It is fair, the family agrees, that my sister doesn't care much for me. I have had several accidents. Falls, crashes, bonks, it goes on. I have had several accidents, and, as a response or cause, drink. I do not like the tuxedo my sister picked for me. I do like the crowd, the combed hairdos, the teenaged country club bartenders, their Long Island teas.

"I have forgotten my shoes," my sister laments, "and you, Boris, must retrieve them. Deliver them posthaste. Do not fuck this up." And so, because I must blow-start my car, and right now, after teas, cannot blow-start my car, because of the imperative *Do not fuck this up*, I must bribe Mr. Wang Song, our old ag. sci. teacher, to let me borrow his car, which is the ceremonial car, a fancy black I-don't-know-what with *Just Married*, and cans tied to it, and et cetera.

Mr. Wang Song is shrewd. Mr. Wang Song is shrewd enough to recognize me. Mr. Wang Song is shrewd enough to recognize in me demons, flaws, to diagnose young men with stutters, with yips (Always he says, Boris, you have the yips), to refuse me his keys but let me ride shotgun.

Mr. Wang Song and I cruise along I-35 with the top down. His tie flutters behind him like a dog's tongue. "Big day," Mr. Wang Song admits, and I agree: rarely am I trusted to save weddings. "Not for you," Mr. Wang Song corrects, "for the Gourd Queen."

My sister is the Gourd Queen. My sister is the Gourd Queen of Schertz, Texas. My sister once completed a maize maze faster than we other children, carved a flawless jack-o'-lantern, baked a sumptuous pumpkin pie, was awarded a plaque reading Gourd King/Queen. Deservedly so. I entered the same maze, transfixed by the mastery of its creation: the high corn walls, fine green-brown hairs on each tuft, hay bales where one might rest, contemplate structure, the mind of the labyrinth's maker. But I equivocated at every turn. Dusk lowered. Parents and children sang my name like cheesing a rat: *Bo-ris, Bo-ris, Bo-ris.*

And me, fool that I am, mistook their chanting for triumph, for love. And me, fool that I am, spoke my own name this way, when trying not to stumble an introduction: *Bo-ris, I am Bo-ris.*

A whole life can be this way. Some blaze forth while you stutter, you guess, you pick your thigh mole through your pocket and wonder, Who is right, Who cares to catch you, Which shoe is the right shoe, and How will I go on?

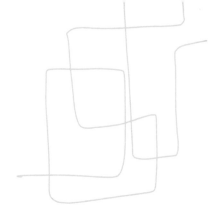

# MAſTⒺRPLANſ

Sheena sits beside Sid on the waterbed and dictates an essay on the panoptical impulse behind deer blinds. It occurred to her last week, during a phone call with her brother Frank about his most recent population-control hunting trip: How ethically inclined hunters consider themselves the wardens of the natural world (some even use the word *warden*), and how those ridiculous tree houses for grown men are structurally akin to watchtowers in prisons. Because Sheena has only one flesh-and-blood arm—the other: a transradial prosthetic that attaches below the elbow and features a stainless steel hook—Sid thuds out her words on their shared laptop. This is their nightly ritual. Finger by finger, Sid uses the hunt-and-kill method of typing, locating each key before pressing it, while nibbling a cinnamon-sugar Pop-Tart.

A few crumbs spill from his mouth when he asks her to define *calamitous*.

"Ah," he says, bolus of Pop-Tart showing, "as in, your professor's party was calamitous."

It really was. Before all else, Sheena is learning in her new role as a literary studies doctoral candidate and aspiring ecocritic, she must always make clear that it's okay to shake left hands, or to skip hand-shakes altogether. She's not wild for hugs. She'd prefer you don't find a way to enlist her in the dinner prep, because, no, there isn't a task that's particularly breezy with a hook. She cannot dice the onion, and, no, that's not a decision she'd like to negotiate—she's accepted the finality of cannot. She cannot shave the fennel. She'd rather cross her legs and small-talk while you grapple with the recipe. She can pour herself a second glass of wine, no problem.

Why the hook? Are there not robotic hands, here in the future? There are, yes, and she's looked into them, but when she can hardly afford a dental cleaning on her grad school insurance plan, how do you propose she pay for a bionic arm that'll let her drum the bongos? So, it's the trusty hook, which she's been using almost all of her life and can rely on.

In her old circles, Sheena never had to lay out ground rules. Old school friends held barbecues and marijuana-intensive potlucks in rented cabins. They used her hook as a blunt-pinching device, had her remove the prosthesis, peel off the sweaty sleeve, and they passed her artificial arm around like a forceps, the silver hook pinching the blunt trailed by its thin slip of smoke. Not her new colleagues. These people required drag-out transparency, every interpersonal hang-up expressed, then accommodated, until an evening of rustic grain salad and lambswool sweaters felt more like pirouetting through one of those only-in-the-movies laser beam security systems—Do not trip the alarm. They wanted to know the rules, the framework of how to be around someone with a hook, but out of spite or laziness or any number of less obvious indecencies, Sheena wouldn't address it, hasn't. It might do them some good, she'd thought sitting with her wine, to have a little rub against the unknown.

All night at the party, Sid was no help. Never a chute out of social awkwardness, Sid; rather, he was a trapdoor into it. He found her colleagues neutered and funny. Tonging himself a second load of greens, he announced to the table that he was thinking of applying to their program, too, that he was mapping a dissertation on feline anality.

"You think Freud was ass-obsessed," he'd said, "you should meet Pickles."

Sid isn't sure why he said this, except that it occurred to him, and he has lived long enough and worked hard enough to say what he pleases. As he types Sheena's essay, he can't help but feel like her outlook is the exact opposite, that she's learning a whole new language from these academic stiffs, one that's annexing continents in her brain. It's a language, of course, he cannot speak, and he senses this nightly homework typing is some kind of regimented exposure to the fact that she's evolving right past him: Sheena holding his head in front of all he is not and cannot be.

When he shares this sentiment with her, she doesn't respond.

Homework lasts until bedtime, when he moves her laptop to the floor, unbuckles his Wranglers, and tackles her back onto the waterbed. They like to start each romp with a gasp, and this time Sid gets one, a moment later, as he attempts a rolling bra-removal that plunges Sheena's hook into the liner of their waterbed.

For a moment they lie there, backsides becoming wet. Water pools around them. Dimly, it gurgles. The usual quietness of their house is replaced with the gurgle. Their clothes begin to soak.

Like any sharp metal object, Sheena's hook has always possessed the potential to destroy. She has accidentally destroyed curtains, book jackets, and once, a television screen. At her cousin's baby shower, the fox terrier jumped into her lap and foolishly she reached to halt it with the wrong hand. She had to excuse herself, and as she scuttled out the whole room followed her with their eyes. But the waterbed was supposed to be different. For years they'd taken priestly care not to do exactly this, the simple math of hook plus bed obvious. She removes the hook to sleep. She removes the hook to have sex. She removes the hook from the waterbed liner, and water comes more intensely from a dark green gash. It spills over the bed onto the closed top of her computer.

"Is it, like, hooked to a hose or something?" Sid asks, agog. "It keeps coming."

Sheena rushes to the bathroom and starts up the blow-dryer to save the laptop. Sid empties the linen closet, the laundry baskets, every dishtowel and grease rag, bathmat, and at the last second, a chair cushion, and forms a turret around the bed. He wonders if they'd overfilled it somehow. A mess he would've expected, but this? Calamitous. He feels it's his responsibility to repair their feelings, to ply the air with jokes; he hollers across the room, "Didn't think I'd get you this wet!"

Over the whir of the blow-dryer, Sheena cannot hear him, and this, he thinks, may be for the best.


Frank Gilkey sleeps in his Dodge. This will be the night of the waterbed incident. But before that there's the truck's grumpy idle, the heater, the sports talk radio through the speakers: a story about the third-string weakside linebacker, the university he attended, the courage he derives from overcoming a stutter.

Jersey Lilly is Asian fusion, sake cocktails, and heady, salty soups. Humongous rooftop electric water lilies cast a blue haze over everything; the blue light in gauzy tangents stretches across on the truck's windshield. Before he fell asleep, Frank felt like he was inside an egg.

Sleep: the day's only reward. More and more, Frank feels life has broken its promise with him, the one that says: with time comes an expanding of things, plurality, relationships, grandchildren, et cetera. Instead, the opposite is true. The older he gets, daily, the fewer things he has to access. There's his work—a suddenly boutique contracting company, since mega-developers have shouldered into the county—and there's his favorite restaurant with its pho and ramen, there's his sports radio, and there's his sister Sheena. Sloppy, near-midnight meals are unrepresented in the grief cycle. No one told him. No one said, "Charlotte will die and mourning will be talk radio and tables for one. That is how you'll get to sleep."

The combination is killer. Edamame and two shaken sake cocktails, then soup and a cold Tsingtao. Add in the local sports radio station and you've got an especially sedative brew. Booze, salt, and nonthreatening arguments—all the passion and none of the consequence. Repetitive topics, teams Frank knows with expert intimacy. The hosts range from piggish to overexuberant—that had been Charlotte's position anyway. Why listen to this? How can you like this? Questions she never vocalized but intimated with a shrewd downcast of her eyebrow whenever she climbed in his truck and the radio came chittering to life. Sometimes, at the end of his commute, he'd change the dial to the classic rock station before killing the engine, just in case he and Charlotte needed to take a nighttime ride to the grocery store for some forgotten ingredient. Now he rarely cooks. Another offcut, another facet of daily life lost in the narrowing.

His phone wakes him with a resounding ping. It's a text from his sister, then a call from her live-in boyfriend, Sid. They've sprung a leak in the waterbed. He uh-huhs his way through the conversation, fiddles with the volume knob on the radio, scratches electric-yellow mustard off his jeans. Sid describes a flood. Sometimes they find excuses to enlist him in this or that, he knows, to distract him, to get him out of the house. But he doesn't have the energy to pick around for truths, so Frank agrees to stop over and take a look.

Water has spread from Sid and Sheena's bedroom all the way to Frank's feet at the door when he enters without a knock. It arcs off the bed in all directions. He notices the water does not rush out the open door behind him but instead resists the doorway, pooling in the center of the room—is the floor bowed? Some trick of surface tension? There isn't time to measure. He hurries in with his wet/dry vac, the one he's repaired four times, and does not greet his sister as she taps the keyboard of a non-responsive laptop. He places the vacuum down next to Sid, who is on his hands and knees trying to contain the flood.

"Is this you?" Frank asks. "You did this?"

Sid points to Sheena and says, "Yargh."

The force with which water pours from the bed mesmerizes Frank.

"Did you replace the liner?" Frank says to Sheena. "You have to replace the liner every year. Six months, even. You can't overfill it."

"We didn't touch it," Sheena says, "except when we popped it."

Frank lays his hand on the mattress and gives it a press; it feels fully plump, like a belly or a biceps. "I told you to replace it. Every year, I said. At least."

Sid starts up the vacuum and guides its floppy hose along the bedposts.

"There was nothing wrong with the liner," Sheena says. "How many years old is it?"

"I don't know how many years!" Sid says.

Frank hurries outside to his pickup and digs through the heap of junk in the bed for anything, anything at all. Tape. In the truck bed is a hodgepodge of gear, mostly the components of an airplane kit. He moves aside the chalky tip of a carbon-fiber wing flap, the unassembled gears of a captain's chair. His rubber waders hide amidst the junk. Charlotte wouldn't have allowed his truck to get like this. Charlotte was raised by her father, a docent at the Eldred World War II Museum, a mothball of a man whom Frank sometimes meets for lunch when he's out toward Turtlepoint. Her childhood home was utterly museum-like, a haven for spillover exhibits, maps and artifacts awaiting rotation. Frank liked how Charlotte brought a backbone of cleanliness to their own home, that by law of their marriage all of his tools had a predetermined place. It was moneysaving too, the organization she inspired. Charlotte kept the books for his contracting company, and under her scrupulous accounting, their bottom line limped out of the red. When Frank turned forty-five, they'd been able to afford their first vacation, a trip to Turks and Caicos where they spent as much time on the humid beach, in their hotel Jacuzzi, as they did in a wobbly little Cessna, flying from island to island. Frank watched Charlotte stare down at the ocean going by, her forehead pressed to the window and headset mussing up her hair, and he knew she was transcending somehow, that she'd found something in that small machine in the sky.

As he trudges back inside, Frank has the once-a-day realization that there are so many aspects of Charlotte he'll never get to discuss with anyone: enough wine and she'd sing, the dimples over her bum, the smell of a certain sea salt product she sprayed in her hair.

The water has risen. It's a wading pool contained, somehow, by the house: The physics of door jambs, air vents, cracks in the floorboards do not apply. A tide rising. Still, the mattress appears completely full. Frank scratches. Doesn't make sense. Leaning over the bed, he tries to patch the hole with tape, but the water dampens the adhesive. He peers into the gash. It's too opaque to see into; water flows steadily.

He cannot seal the bed. He cannot fix an unfixable thing.

On hands and knees, Sid works the vacuum, water approaching his thighs. He wonders how much the vacuum's tank can hold, how long this whole episode will take, still a little hazy from the missed opportunity to make love and worried Frank can read that on his face. He thinks, Prince or P-Funk, something with a strut, the whole episode better if set to music. It could be cinematic.

Sheena has begun removing valuables from the bedroom— books mostly, fat with peeling barcodes, these books she needs more than a car, a toothbrush, although she really only has time to read the introductions. Before her admittance to the university, she managed a regional team of cleaning women and oversaw the disposal of 950 pounds of paper towel in less than a year. One foggy and humorless morning she came across that figure in her purchasing spreadsheet and dropped egg salad in her lap. For weeks she begged her team to fold each paper towel before using it to wipe up, but they just thought she was being cheap. Her admissions essay was on interstitial suspension, using the metaphor of the folded paper towel to represent the conceptual space between humans and a way-out-there everything else, the unreachable environment. Looking back, the paper was embarrassing, clunky, just enough to get her in, and although her stipend is breadcrumbs, she loves that she will never again have to contact another homeowner and recite the lost property clause, she will never again demand to search the purse of an employee, she will never have to come home after dark, hair smelling like turpentine, to scrutinize the trash can for compostables while Sid watches, liable at any moment to call her insane.

"Is it possible it's coming faster?" Sid yells over the vacuum.

"We can move the bed out," Frank suggests.

The men squat on each side of the bed and try to lift it. They cannot. The waterbed is so much more voluminous than Sheena ever knew, and because of her hook, she has no choice but to help in the least helpful ways. She delivers Frank a bottle of water, and, looking at what she's done, has to leave the house to keep from screaming.

The night is familiar with stars. None of this makes any sense.

Hypothesis: Humans map their miseries upon a graph of space and time, so when a single unfortunate event takes place, other data points nearby seem to corelate. Our sadnesses appear to group when, most likely, pain is random, but we cannot resist the urge to make it constellate, so our lives might mimic the natural world, the shapes made by stars.

Frank doesn't see it that way. Sheena knows he doesn't, and she resents him for it. To him, everyone has a single and definitive trauma, and life ripples out from there. When she was seven, Sheena was bit by a snake in the woodsy swamp behind their grandfather's house in St. Augustine. Thirty minutes before, Frank had declared they'd go exploring, and though forbidden from crossing the backyard line, he gladly trooped straight into the archway of spruce pine armed with a single sharpened stick. They spent the afternoon searching for snakes. The horrific news was that they found one: a cottonmouth tucked in a palmetto thicket. Frank staggered back as if pulled by a string; Sheena went right up to it, entranced, and reached for the most authentic thing she'd ever seen. She said, *I'm sorry, Frank, Frankie, I'm sorry,* as they felt their way back through the swamp, flinching at every stick that snapped underfoot, Frank's belt tight around her biceps. By the time they emerged, Sheena's arm was the color of jacaranda blooms. It was the defining trauma of her life. And, for a time, this too was Frank's, but it would be replaced. He would be forty-five. Charlotte would be taking a flying lesson at the Doylestown Airport. He would get a phone call while driving, while listening to arguments about sports. After, he would sleep more than he could've predicted: blackly, utterly, a step outside the slipstream of time.

His whole graph would rearrange.


With Sheena outside, Frank considers a series of possible solutions, patches, ways to put it back together. Plans. Plans have always been his curse. In grade school art, he was a disaster. He never found pleasure in movies—how do people sit when there's so much to do? It was Charlotte's position that his ability to repair things was an art form, though usually it felt like a malfunction in his brain. Honestly, it was easier to think about ways to repair inconsequential things: the molding around the kitchen ceiling, the Eagles, ways to improve their run game.

In a few minutes, when she returns, the water is high enough to touch Sheena's shins. Still it gushes, it flumes. She eyes her brother. Does Frank somehow know the bed was punctured in a bout of friskiness? She wonders if his loneliness makes this a crime, that asking him over to help was an aggression too micro for her to realize. The bed had belonged to their parents, and, most likely, had been host to both of their conceptions. Some nights, the idea of sex with Sid on it makes her queasy. She thinks this might be the Freudian link, that as the sexual throne of their parents drains, she subconsciously wants to be with Frank, to be in the presence of family. But she's never read Freud, and if she doesn't get all her books off the floor, she'll never get the chance to.

She carries a stack of books to the kitchen table, the bottommost dripping. *Heart of Darkness* looks as though its fictional river has overrun its pages. She watches down the hall as her brother and Sid try once more to lift the bed, wonders how all this water can keep coming, and blinks, as if the right number of blinks will make everything as it should be.

Only a queen mattress, and still, somehow, all this water. What kind of conservationist, she begins, but will not allow herself to finish the thought. She can see the impossible overflow is a missive, the laughing universe with one more tragedy for her to decode.

Sid carries the vacuum outside and dumps its contents. Frank paces in and out of the room until Sheena catches his eye and they look at one another helplessly, his hands tucked behind his head. Until three years ago, Sheena's life had been the considerably more tragic one. She's been the sufferer, the one with the identifiable trauma. Frank managed to age into a rocky, handsome man and married an irresponsibly svelte woman who was ass-over-elbows in love with him in all his sawdusty glory. Sheena, on the other hand, bounced from shipwreck boyfriend to boyfriend until she met Sid, who she's been with for half a decade and loves in equal measure to good guacamole. Instead of a wedding, they spent their savings on this house in the woods, which is quickly filling with water.

The men trade positions, try to lift the bed once more, but cannot. Frank works the vacuum while Sid grabs trash from around the room—tube socks, an unfinished crossword, a bag of spent Burger King he'd hid under the bed—and tries to plug the hole with it.

"Don't do that!" Frank hollers above the vacuum. "You'll tear it open!"

"I dunno, man, these are unconventional times!"

Sid tosses the trash and holds his hands over the hole. Water geysers between his fingers. Although Frank has always presented himself as superior, Sid knows what he's doing. Sid admires his own confidence. His intuition has always been his gift. He knew Bush would level Baghdad, he felt a tingling on his neck the day Philip Seymour Hoffman died, and he somehow predicted that he himself would blow the lead in the final inning of the final game of the '88 Little League World Series, that he'd return with his silent teammates to a hotel in Williamsport, Pennsylvania, while one room over Team Japan roared in delight, that he'd have to watch himself repeat the mistake—a hanging fastball, just above the batter's belt—on ESPN feeds for years, each time looking into his own childhood face, and wondering, Why? What now? and, Will I ever move on?

But using hands to plug the hole cannot stop the water.

The flooding is almost above the low windowsills. From outside, the house resembles an aquarium in progress. Why it isn't leaking out, escaping beneath the doors, no one knows. Sheena must fight the urge to design a thesis in her mind about the commerciality of a bed made to mimic the impossible sensation of sleeping on water, how the body yearns for a simulation of what might seem natural but could never be.

"Any other ideas?"

"We can try to reroute the water. You have a garden hose?"

"Round back," Sheena says.

"Get it, Sid," Frank says.

"Why Sid?" Sid says.

"Get it, Sid," Sheena says.

The older you get, the more things you can fairly describe as haunting. The loss of Sheena's limb, in Frank's mind, has always been an unfixable problem. He'd been the older brother by fifteen months, and where he could've pulled her away from the palmetto thicket, he'd stayed back, frozen, and watched. He hated himself for that stupor, the way his legs locked, as they would again decades later at the mailbox when he received the first piece of Charlotte's Piper PA-34 Seneca, wrapped in packing paper with sharpie notes on folded schematics. The package was from a lawyer in Harrisburg who wanted Frank to participate in a multidistrict litigation. He unwrapped it: a chunk of steel and hose. First Frank felt its heft in his hands, then the crush of realization: This thing had been so close to her in her last minutes. It outlived her. For weeks the chunk sat on the kitchen table. It smelled cindery. He felt it staring at him as he had his morning coffee, its sooty face watching him when he came in late from Jersey Lilly and flopped on the couch. Once, very late at night, a little tipsy, Frank arrived home and could've sworn he heard the piece of motor chime, as if accusing him of something. Of listening to too much radio, of drowning out the onslaught of his own brain. He hadn't heard it speak, not necessarily, but there it was, on a bed of newspaper on the table where they used to eat, illuminated by lamplight, demanding something.

Frank studied a few web pages and learned about kit planes: small, DIY assemblages of parts and plans to construct an airplane. Perhaps the answer was to buy one, to someday take a cathartic flight that traced Charlotte's last. But that was too expensive, and too easy. He had no desire to go back into the sky. Not ever. He waited to see if additional pieces would come from the lawyer's office. The legality was fuzzy to him. Were bits of Charlotte's plane not evidence? Why were they sent to, of all people, him? He phoned the lawyer's office and sat listening to hypnotic jazz for twenty minutes before deciding the entire thing was a ruse.

When he mentioned all of this to Sheena (and, by proxy, Sid) they formed their own theories, but none were satisfying. It seemed sad at first, pathetic next, then a little insane. But when the next part arrived, and as he compulsively read internet articles about its function, Frank began to consider himself capable of building something, of resurrecting something. It was a loop: lunacy, wonderment, meaning. He discovered that the first piece on the kitchen table fit between the fuel line and timing chain; the second piece was a scorched scrap of bulkhead. When he understood the useful purpose of each part, Frank felt a feeling he could not describe, like putting down a heavy suitcase he didn't know he'd been carrying. Then there was a stretch of only bills in the mail. It seemed to Frank that the lawyer had given up, moved on to other husbands, widowed wives. He moved both airplane parts from the kitchen to the shed.

Then a package came. A shred of instrument panel. The next week, a landing gear stay. Frank trembled at the impossibility, the stupid way he felt he had to keep this all a secret. But it was also impossible not to wonder which bit of machinery slid into which, and which piece, for Charlotte, had been the culprit, which point of schema had gone wrong. One morning he blew off work and spent the day in his shed attempting to link whatever he could, brake piston to pressure plate, wing bracket to scorched fuselage. Charlotte was never a Jesus person, but she had the habit of uttering inspirational little aphorisms whenever their lives felt hairy and sad. "There's some purpose to this," she'd say, or, "Wait and see how it works in the long run." But Frank couldn't feel the long run, not anymore. In God terms, the airplane, the snake in the thicket, the lawyer were all steps in the masterplan. But Frank wondered if the lawyer was placed in his life as a patch, a temporary and immediate fix, God delivering a mystery to keep him from sticking his head in the oven. He hauled all the lumber out of his shed to clear space, buttressed sawhorses with cinder blocks to make a plywood table. Deep into the night he tinkered or read until he was too hungry to keep on. He'd drag himself out and before unplugging the extension cord to the shed's work light, glance back at his framework of aircraft. Some nights it looked to him like the bones of a dinosaur, excavated, a creature flight. Sometimes he recognized the altar: the steps, the canopy, the table, the gearwork of a saint. Then he'd tug the cord from its socket and make it all go black.

Sid stops before reentering the house to take his turn looking up at the sky. Constellations: ask Sid, and he'd tell you he couldn't name one, would rather make up his own. He wasn't one for memorizing mnemonics, invisible shapes, other people's gropes at controlling what's unknown.

The muddy hose is snaked around Sid's limbs, and, because he knows Sheena reads the world more closely than others, he coils the hose to make it look less like a snake. The work dirties his hands and takes a while, but it's fine. It's fine to take a while, he has learned, in doing almost anything. The hole in the bed is not going to be fixed, not even by whatever magic Frank thinks can be accomplished with a garden hose. Sid knows that Frank is, truthfully, not tremendously skilled in the field of mechanics. He is much better at working with wood. Still, Frank is constantly fiddling under the hood of his Dodge, or rewiring the guts of a vacuum, and Sid sees nothing wrong with that. People need to fool themselves. They need to waste time. He's done it. There is a windowless massage parlor on Lower Stump Road where he goes to sometimes feel love. He knows it's fake.

He knows that Maxine, with her two bearlike hands, also knows the love she provides is fake. And in their mutual knowledge there is silence, there is agreement, and Maxine serves as provider of distraction. All people need this, Sid knows. He just knows.

"What now?" he says when he comes inside, the hose neat in his arms, and the water, unfathomably, still gushing. Soon they'll have to leave or else drown.

"Put one end through the window," Frank says, "the other in the hole."

Sid pops out the window screen and drapes the hose over the sill. He plunges the other end into the mattress hole. It doesn't change a thing. The water is almost at their knees, and each, though it is unspoken between them, is becoming too tired to care about this mystery, too confused to suss this out. Previously unseen things float on the surface: a mousetrap, a mini-golf scorecard, a destroyed printout of *Slow Violence and the Environmentalism of the Poor*.

"Do you think we're being punished for something?" Sid asks.

No one responds.

Frank's mind wanders to the Phillies: Will they make any moves at the trade deadline? Sheena considers the difference between blackholes, which absorb, and this hole, which exudes. Sid watches these people, his cobbled family, in their distraction, and repeats the question only to be ignored again.

This always happens to Sid, either at the office or at home. At some imperceptible point in the day, everyone stops listening to him. They cease to acknowledge anything he says. But Sid doesn't just suspect they're being punished. He knows it. Because he knows things. He just does. For instance, he knows that the bed will keep overflowing, that in some way, their time has come. It will never stop. He knows that they'll pack for the night and follow Frank back to his house where they'll park behind the shed. He knows, peering in on that skeletal assembly of airplane, he will see that

Frank does not yet have a steering wheel, that no propeller is bolted to the nosey tip.

Sid will rip the steering wheel from the neighbor kid's ATV, will hit the junk shop where they sell lawn-ornament windmills for a rusty prop, and when he greases them up a bit, when he hits them with a torch, they will look authentic, and Frank will find another box at his doorstep, he will open it, and he will be stolen from grief. He will think there's an answer.

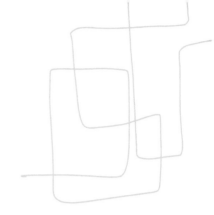

# CAN YOU PAINT A SMILE?

Because of her tumor, my mother's decided to audition morticians though she is not officially dying; I am, according to all available measures. This ache near my liver, a sensation that the room is shrinking. I am thirty-five, my mother seventy-one. Affairs in order was her rationale: "Who's picking for me? Your sister? You?" Now we're waiting nervously for Brassly of Brassly Funeral Home & Service to find us in the foyer, my mother transferring candies from the bowl to her purse.

Brassly regrets to say there are no discounts for the still-living, but her beautification's on the house.

My mother, a candy pocketed in her cheek, wiggles with excitement.

Also confirming death: the odor of mothballs, formaldehyde, a room behind us we cannot enter because it holds a dead man. We're led by Brassly through a dim parlor and two more rooms (one expensive, one cheap) with their rows of mourners' chairs, caskets, and lecterns for eulogizing. I follow quietly behind my mother, khakis suffocating my thighs.

Only I, at times, understand my mother's death to be deliberate, that she's tired of her knees and civilization and pleasantries in the grocery store and rumpled shirts from the dryer and roof leaks above the bed. Every morning fantastically the topmost blanket is dry and she thinks: Of all the days, this is a good one for an off-duty army captain to saunter by, or for Azrael to appear trumpeting beside the water stain on her ceiling.

Brassly looks grateful, near excited, as we help my mother onto a rolling bed and he lowers a magnifying glass and light to her face. He says: "So what are we aiming for, dear? Understated? Timeless? Something youthful? And these bags..."

Possibilities smolder behind her eyelids, my mother: yearning for any furnace of interest, of love. Today it is raining, but tomorrow she'll retell Brassly's tawdry makeover and flirtation as we sweat, agreeing it's fair to call him a capitalist, her twirling a prawn in the largest periwinkle room of Logan's Restaurant. I shouldn't be harsh. Perhaps it's just the room, perfumed with flambéed wine and butter. Perhaps it's the gulls throating worms beside the dock. Heretofore I've been a child. Tomorrow it's Tavossi's, the only funeral home with TVs in their front window; they livestream the wake and tribute for passersby. My mother will get her makeover for free, a clasping of hands, and I will excuse myself here and now to the restroom to sit solemnly still in my pants upon the seat, to look at the four stall walls around me, and try to imagine her life below.

# SMOKE FOR THE MOZARTS

K aren performs for the group. Another dirge. All E and A minor, all heavy-handed with a walkdown in the bass, delivered into the mic with spittle and pop. There's light applause: My students have learned, at least, to be fair. In the back I type comments for each performance and email them immediately: *I know I say reach the back row, but did you reach the front?*

The Mozarts are a musically inclined collection of the delusional and dying who meet in the Presbyterian church on Bridge and Third. All live with a stern belief in his or her deadly illness, though doctors cannot corroborate. It's a burden twice. First you're dying and second you receive nothing: no care, no sympathy, just a referral slip for a psychiatrist and a flyer for our Thursday group, The Mozarts.

Next is Barry. Barry is six foot seven with a wingspan larger than my sofa. He played for the Austin Toros in the NBA's developmental league until a bicycling accident convinced him his right leg was damaged to the point of amputation. The leg is indeed there, massive and pants-clad and as seemingly competent as the other, but still Barry moves with a crutch and reports phantom sensations behind the thigh. He is my most promising student.

Barry's cello looks kindergarten-small between his knees, and Gerta, our only European, assists him on electric keys (Gerta has vitiligo; she swears it's cancer).

The overheads reflect on Barry's bald head, and, yes, I know this is a cliché, but a teacher's job is sometimes to choose which clichés are permissible and which are not. It's also my job to edit, to gently steer, to nudge students in the direction of painful truth, but who am I to edit Barry with his eyebrows plucked into perfect Nike swooshes, who's spent hours and years and possibly one lifetime in empty gyms for nothing, whose polished shoes are larger than the headlights of my car? This group owes Barry. He named us when we had our what's-the-name-gonna-be meeting, taught us that Mozart was dead two weeks before a Berlin newspaper announced he'd been poisoned, though nowadays they think he died of strep. "The greatest musician ever," Barry explained alongside a PowerPoint of baby-faced Mozart done in pastel, "and nobody diagnosed what killed him. They didn't listen to his symptoms. And this was a great man."

We respect Barry but nonetheless when he touches bow to strings there is a commotion in the middle aisles. Two Mozarts are fretting. Murmurs abound.

"Excuse us," I say, but they are standing, flailing.

"We smell smoke," Ron Christmas says. "Tina and me both. Who else smells it?"

It's difficult to describe the tremble in Ron Christmas's voice when he asks, *Who else smells it?* Because of course he has to worry— Ron, whose salivary gland overproduces because of rabies and is constantly wiping his chin though nothing is there.

"Got zilch back here. Let's hear Barry," I say.

"I smell it!" says Tina (hypersensitive to power lines).

"There are many things in the world to smell," Barry agrees into the mic.

"Please," and I am slapping my palms. "My wife's elbows deep with grad school work, she's got both kids, I'd like to—"

"There is," announces Karen, rising and pointing, "smoke!"

The hubbub swells. Gerta paces to and fro on stage, sniffs the curtains.

"Enough!" I say, and am pacing the aisle to commandeer the mic. "You may not derail this performance for undetected, nonexistent—"

"Wait!" Barry calls into the mic. For a moment, the room's his. He points to the side door where Mrs. Waterson, the front desk person, stands with her bag on her shoulder.

"Apologies for interrupting," Mrs. Waterson says, "but the church is on fire. The kitchen. A microwave. If you could—"

But it's too late: The sprinkler system kicks on. It showers over us, dampening the chairs, our laps. Mrs. Waterson splits. I make for my laptop. But down in the rows The Mozarts do not exit.

Emergency lights flash. There's an alarm like frightened elephants.

The Mozarts rise, expressions buoyant, and converge at the stage to confirm one another: Karen, Tina, Barry, Gerta, Ron. You were right, they say, a handshake, a hand on a shoulder, Karen's hand slipping into Ron's (a moment I am not supposed to see). You were right, she says and dabs his chin for him.

Water's collecting in the instrument cases, atop the organ. Soon the fire company will drape foil blankets on The Mozarts, EMTs will check pulses and listen to their breathing, and soon they will herd back toward the exits, all but Karen and Ron, who are still getting soaked, still dabbing, still repeating: You were, I was, we are.

# HOW TO SHOOT GROOMS

### 6:30–8:30 The Rehearsal Dinner

It was Lucas's idea of a sick joke to ask you to photograph his wedding, and it was your idea of a joke to say yes. Two years divorced and he's still cheap. Two years divorced, and you've nearly convinced yourself this is sane. Lucas's last name is Sane, and, this time, you wish you were joking. To this day it's still your last name—Sane. Why not change it? Well, you changed it once. You became Mel Sane. And how'd that work out? Plus, you won't give Lucas the satisfaction of un-sullying the Sane name. You don't itch to be a Reifschneider again.

New photographers: it's best not to title your business with a marital last name. When you leave him, you'll have to redo your website. LLCs aren't easily retitled, or maybe they are—you haven't tried—but Sane Photography, objectively, sounds bad.

When you arrive at the venue, get to know your fellow vendors. Offer to help those hectically setting tables. Chum around. Network. The florist, for instance, may ask if it's true what they're saying, that you're the groom's ex-wife. If Brent the bartender believes your lie that you've never tried Jägermeister, take one shot with him, then take one more.

When shooting grooms, remember women marry men for a variety of reasons. Your job is to find what's handsome in a groom, no matter how slouchy or combed-over. Dig out his kindness, notice the gap in his smile. Remember your own men. There were times when love was like a warm-blooded animal who slept between you, a thing so glass-boned you could roll over and crush it. Recall being held. Ask yourself, why do mammals live so long, and find the answer is arms.

Lucas arrives in his wrinkled golf shirt. You've laundered that shirt. You've forgotten that shirt in the dryer, long after the buzz, and let it go to wrinkles. You've never felt anything for that shirt but a bored hatred and you'll be rolled in dung before you feel anything for it now.

Photographers: take time to spruce your groom before shooting him. When he's around his groomsmen, he'll not be seen piecing back his cowlick or fussing with his tuck. It isn't that he's inattentive as much as he's self-conscious about being self-conscious. Men can be this way. Lucas *is* this way. Even now your hands are coursing toward his waist to untuck and dewrinkle. Let professionalism stop you.

"Mel," he says as you approach, your name spoken with the flat surprise people use when identifying roadside wildlife. He kisses your cheek. "I half-thought you wouldn't show."

Have a rapport with clients, never hide what makes you *you*.

"Fix yourself," you say, and flick a furrow in his shirt.

Lucas's bride is a sunburned Dallas restaurant heiress, or so you gather from chitchat as you photograph her and Lucas at the head of a long table. Know (and shoot) the key players. Avoid what others avoid in themselves. The cross-armed sister keeps her flab hidden. The aunt has a glass eye. No need to avoid Lucas's mother: you both know you are here.

Capture details. Mint table runners. A flower threaded in a grandmother's hair. Here and again raise your lens to those who deliver toasts. Later, edit out their sweat the same way they, now, edit you from Lucas's life, retold as a screwball comedy coursing around goofs and bumps (i.e., you) until Lucas arrives at destiny, which will happen tomorrow, when he marries the correct someone else.

Feel his mother's gaze, the phantom sensation of her grip on your throat as she grips her scotch. She is a woman who once told you your sickness was hard on her, on Lucas, and asked, *How much is even real?*

Do not run to the bathroom. Remember: you control time. You halt it by bending your finger.

Lift your camera. Click.

Check focus. Click. Move on.

## 2:00–4:00 The Getting Ready

Your job is to know the standard moments. Bride and bridesmaids in robes. Bride's mother zipping the dress. Bride at her vanity, head cocked, considering her hair.

Lucas's mother is a clenched woman with cavernous black eyes and a mahogany dye job that has always made you think of movie theater licorice. "Oh," she says when she sees you, and steps out of the shot, so she can keep moving, so she can extol the bride's beauty to a nearby aunt.

Oh. Mouth a circle, a zero, an aperture.

Aim. Click.

After long stretches without hearing from Lucas, his mother would call you, to dig out why he didn't love her by free election. When it became clear that your marriage was a thing made with cracks, his mother stopped calling you and began calling him—she flattened herself like a mouse and slipped in. Later you told yourself that one good thing came from your divorce: a mother and child reunion.

Get comfortable with people walking into you, with your objecthood. There's nothing wrong with it. What you've already anticipated cannot surprise you, and most everything at a wedding has already been anticipated by each guest, except that there will be a human—a stranger, usually—behind the camera.

If you've contracted a second photographer, she will spend these hours shooting the groom. Warn her of what she may encounter in the groom and groomsmen's readying room: golf buddies, Red Bull, Bulleit Rye. Men will undress shamelessly in front of her. Most are oblivious. Others will like it.

## 4:30–5:30 The Ceremony

In sickness and in health. The fast and dirty—
Is the ceremony Jewish, Hindu, Catholic? Get the kiss; it's all anyone cares about.

The bride enters with a brother (or perhaps an older son) at her side, and Lucas appears nonplussed. You know his expressionlessness doesn't mean he's unfeeling because he's told you. He's overwhelmed. What a luxury to be that, *overwhelmed.*

Photographers: you are not beholden to order. Remember that later, when you edit these photographs, when you rearrange the story—the photo of her coming down the aisle is to be followed by the groom's face swollen with love, even if that moment truthfully came just before, when he looked at the flower girl, or at his mother. No one will know you made this change, this small lie. In fact, they expect it. Other lies: do not show the alcoholics already red-faced. Do not capture divorced family members in the same shot.

The smaller you make the lies, the bigger the tip.

The bride makes her way; her train sweeps the petals.

Throughout the ceremony, bride and groom will angle themselves towards the priest or officiant, backs stupidly to the camera. Migrate. Accommodate. The bride will cry thoughtfully, a tear or two thumbed away before her makeup runs. The groom will bawl nauseatingly or not at all.

Lucas describes himself as *sensitive.* You once hated him for that word, the selfishness of it. *Sensitive*: your immune system, one summer day, became sensitive to something but they couldn't tell what. Lucas left you in the emergency waiting room, because, as he said, he felt diseases blowing down on him from the air vents. You didn't see him again for nine days. *You are the one who is cruel,* he would tell you. *You and your words.* Because why? Because you'd told him, later, that he'd replaced his mother with you, remade you into an overbearing, over loving, burdensome presence, and all you ever wanted was plain love. Standard, non-hazardous love, love like vanilla yogurt. You never kept apron strings and told him so—that he had ignored his mother into oblivion and was recreating the conditions with his wife, turning you into the source of his woundedness, his only last action obviously to just disappear.

You do not know words to be cruel. You know them as creatures who spawn once and fall to the ground to die.

In sickness and in health.

Visually, little changes as the priest speaks. Find mothers, grand-mothers. This moment is theirs. You may get lucky: there are no personalized vows. You may get unlucky: the bride wrote a poem. Move across the room. Line her up over Lucas's shoulder. Choose a large aperture to put him out of focus. Drill in on her eye and focus. Pull back. Reframe. Scroll through what you've shot. Lucas's bride's sunburned face is motionless, made up, as it will be when she is dead. Remember this as you shoot her. Remember this as you slide past two hundred iterations of that face.

The thrift store book on photography, the one Lucas bought you, had a fading calfskin cover and an odor like onion soup. Remember Lucas's groan when he read, "All photographs show our deaths." Remember rereading and rereading that sentence in your hospital bed, because Lucas put that book in bag he packed you, the one you had to beg him to bring after he never came back into the emergency waiting room, even after you were examined and admitted. Remember the hospital security guard and nurse, side by side, delivering your bag: *Somebody left it at the front desk.* Remember how death was only a word on a page, acceptable in that way, a thing you could comprehend with ease, until it meant a certain day, a certain hour.

Remember how his phone kept dying, how he never picked up, how after he dropped off the bag, he didn't visit. Remember when, after discharge, you found a different ride home. Remember the backseat of that car. He had already buried you. You couldn't even get that right.

## 5:30–6:30 The Cocktail Hour

Drinks. Canapés. Bring the bride and groom someplace grassy.

Often in evenings a sense of emptiness overcomes you. Dusk phases into night, which phases into memories, real, imagined, and you wish the emptiness would come back, you wish to be scraped clean.

Avoid dreams, their messy shores.

Place yourself between Lucas, his bride, and the lowering sun. Stand far back enough to keep your shadow from splitting them. Zoom. When they're stiff, instruct him to whisper something in her ear, something to make her laugh. Shoot a breath before, when his chin is in her hair, her face expectant.

Yours is this moment, the moment just before.

They assume many poses. As a model, Lucas's bride is cromulent. She disregards the camera, then a few shots later locks in her eyes, she works her posture, she flirts, withdraws, and flattens when you say, "Now a romantic one." Then a pout, and a curl into Lucas's arms.

Then he motion-blurs, swatting at a bee.

Does she know, as you know, that Lucas is allergic to ants, not bees? Does she know that once, drunk and at the moonlit shore, Lucas stripped naked, ran over lawns, and leapt into the San Marcos River? Emerging, he came to you—glistening, screaming a moment later—you don't forget a scream—running back to the shore.

You sat tall and raised your camera, got it all. His akimbo arms and legs, running and swatting. He jumped. Bare assed, over the moon on the river's surface, he was a blue-gray blur. That was the photo you loved most.

Lucas like a scratch and the moon on the river below. The moment just before.

Photographers: know when to leave. Allow bride and groom a moment where you placed them. Let your synthetic moment become their real one.

Walk back over craggy Texas fields. Avoid anthills gravely large.

## 6:30–8:00 The Reception

Their first dance as husband and wife, surprisingly, is a relief, because you're halfway home, halfway to shoes off and a fast shower with the TV volume up, the show with the hot doctor, the one whose patients only he can cure.

Watch her in Lucas's arms and suspect they included dance lessons in their budget. Eighty guests, DJ, barbecue, and what about you? You don't work for free. Photographers: know why you are here. Know what calls you to this work. It could be the freedom of working for yourself, or days alone editing while your partner toils elsewhere, or the satisfaction of a small machine, warm and clicking, in your hands. Is it better to be near love than in it? Is it better outside, where you only feel the heat a thing lets off?

His mother side-eyes you. Flip her the bird.

Their song is "Wonderful Tonight," which you've read is about Eric Clapton, flop haired and grouchy, waiting for his wife to finish getting ready and practicing what he'll say to her when she's finally done. You practiced what you'd say to Lucas when the car dropped you off at home, but his car was gone. The next morning you heard nothing from him. You envisioned car wrecks, heart attacks, and you waited. Essential human work: waiting. You waited for the doctor, waited for results, waited for the drugs to kick in, to wear off. Waited five weeks. Waited for your company's impatience, waited with coffee, tea, made a website for a photography business in all the waiting, are still waiting for a diagnosis.

Stopped waiting for Lucas. Stopped practicing your words. You improved. Your rheumatologist tapered your meds. A text from Lucas: he was so happy to hear.

Shoot the groom.

Shoot his mother.

Shoot the bride.

Shoot her brother, shoot her son.

Shoot a place setting, an untouched plate of food. When it's your turn to eat, eat what's yours. Find a room, a hall, a set of steps outside. Wave the flies off your meat. Eat neatly. Be quick.

Your wedding song was "Your Song." Somewhere, you think, Elton John is still singing, *It's people like you who keep it turned on.* He's talking about the sun, that people keep the sun on. When Ahab couldn't find the whale, he said, *Don't talk to me about blasphemy, I'd punch the sun if it gave offense.* When Lucas couldn't say his reason for leaving, besides *sensitive*, you understood Ahab. Black out the moon, tear down the sun. Planets held by wire in a manmade sky. These things become briefly visible, and you need a minute to think, to consider what's real, if you can find a way to love in the world as you once had.

Watch the blackening horizon. Enjoy each break. Telephone wires stretch and stretch and vanish, and it's still lovely, that metaphor, you decide. It can stay.

### 8:00–10:00 The Dancing, Etcetera.

Some things have no climax.

Lucas's wedding has little passion, no punches. Nary an epiphany, finite glee.

He and his bride are pressed at the forehead. Guests join in dancing: the very old, the very young. Your camera hangs at your neck, and you find yourself disappointed that the bride never glowered at you, her regard for you as a nonthreat one kind of insult. She only gazes into the DJ light, mothlike and stoned.

Do you see yourself in the faces of others?

A wedding represents hard work. Acknowledge that. Consider refraining from booking another so soon. Take a vacation. A long ride in a car with an animal you love. Go on another date with the math teacher. Have sex.

You and Lucas did not have sex on your first night together because you were both deeply, nonfunctionally drunk. You remember this abstention as alive, nearly holy, and you had managed out of your dress in the suite with the curtains open; from the parking lot, a security light shone through the window as white as anything you'd ever seen, and you slept in that light until it switched off and the first traces of sunrise colored the sky from below. You woke up thirsty, filled a wine glass with water in the bathroom, and stood naked at the window. When you were asleep, your heart had been beating so hard it could've killed you. Lucas, corpselike, slept on, and you knew that when your heart did stop, a great and slow unburdening would lessen your weight as if your skin had been a waterlogged shirt. Almost two years later, when Lucas asked for forgiveness, because you did not how else to resuscitate your marriage, you booked the same suite and returned with your groom. Lucas had scheduled his wisdom teeth removal for two days before the trip, and so he spent the whole vacation in and out of consciousness, complaining from the hotel bed for a refill of ice, and you knew this was too late an intervention, the trip, that time had come for comfort measures.

When he was asleep you swiped five painkillers from his orange bottle and at blackest night arranged yourself in a chair in front of that window and swallowed three pills. The security light whitened your neck and arms. The fourth pill you slipped under your tongue after the light went out. The fifth when the sun rose, and you felt nothing, in the end, a divine nothing that offered to erase what filled you before. Where is your nothing now, with its chlorinated water, and the purest white you've ever seen?

Hush.

Find a wall to lean on.

You are almost home.

## 10:00 The Send Off

Outside, under the stars, guests form two lines. The door is at the front of the line, at the other end is you. Sparklers are passed and lit—cedar, cinder, and sulphur. Snap and hiss. In a moment, bride and groom will emerge, move past the sparks, past you, and into a car.

Check your settings. Ready the flash.

Sparklers make faces orange. Adjust. Accommodate. Everyone will cheer but you. You hold still. You are the photographer. Aim. Click. Notice the shutter, how it sounds like the sneeze of something small.

This warm thing in your arms.

The doors are open. The car is waiting.

You've already vanished. You're already gone.

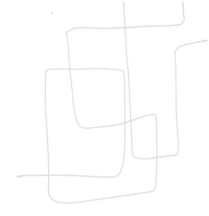

# KICKING TV

I'm finding pieces of you everywhere. Jesus, Terry, your heart in the butter bell? It muttered: Kiss me, big girl. This was, like, 4:00 a.m.. I freaked and splattered my robe with Coke. So I lifted the lid, and there you were, Ter, or at least that fist shaped, purplish, beating part of you, ruining a whole mess of butter.

Your fingers: beneath the couch cushions, writhing, fooling near the hem of my dress. Little onions—like for martinis—that's what I thought I'd found in my cup holder, but they rolled and I knew instantly, the slate-colored irises, the ogling to and fro, with that classic "oh lay an egg" Terry look.

This morning your son missed the bus. I went to shut off the TV in his room and there he was, drumming on your bladder and giggling at what trickled out. We're still working on everything from before: The new speech therapist has hope; he's shown promise with the sax; but he refuses to quit the TV.

For example, just last week, after dinner, everything normal: He's glued to the tube, I'm affixing your femur to your hip. I say, Okay, sport, let's go, shut 'er down, and he doesn't budge. The program is about lions: *Life of Lions*, and, at age six, he is interested in a lion tattoo. So I shut off the TV, and he freaks. I say, Would you like to help? Hand me that tibia. And he puts your leg-bone in his mouth, and romps—romps!—on all fours, announcing himself a tiger.

Tiger? I say. I thought lions were your thing.

Terry the Tiger, he says, and quadrupeds out the front door, toward Tavossi's, because they have TVs in their window display.

We miss you, Terry. Every day, we feel, but rarely speak of, your absence. The two of us, like kooks in this house, an old maid and a little terror, we're making it, we're trying. But, Jesus, listen to me, Ter, you have to please stop with the body parts. Or at least give us some guidance, a little hint, finger a note in the shower steam. Do we reassemble you or throw you away? What parts will you leave next? Toenails were one thing, but a man's anatomy—as a stepmother, I consider myself exempt from certain subjects and explanations.

The TV, though: I can't kick it either. I find myself awake at four every morning, when *Life of Lions* reruns. You'd call it gobble-dygook and put on tea, I know. Pride, Terry. Ain't that a phrase? I lounge with guilt and grief in each palm, and watch till sunrise.

Did I mention your skin slumped in the laundry bin? I pinched your shoulders and lifted you, shook away the socks, and pinned you to our line. When I do dishes, I look out to the yard and watch you. Some days, you sway. Some days, there's mist

**NICK ALMEIDA**'s writing has appeared in or is forthcoming from *Pleiades, American Literary Review, The Southeast Review, Waxwing, Mid-American Review,* and elsewhere. He is a PhD candidate at University of Houston and holds an MFA from The Michener Center for Writers. His chapbook, *Masterplans*, is the grand prize winner of *The Masters Review's* inaugural Chapbook Contest in Fiction, selected by judge Steve Almond.

For more, visit nickalmeida.com.

CPSIA information can be obtained
at www.ICGtesting.com
Printed in the USA
BVHW020343050422
632939BV00003B/9